WHERE'S WALLY?

Completely Crazy

ACTIVITY BOOK

Based on the characters created by

MARTIN HANDFORD

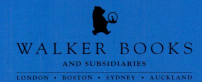

WALKER BOOKS

AND SUBSIDIARIES

LONDON · BOSTON · SYDNEY · AUCKLAND

HI THERE, WALLY-WATCHERS!

TIME FOR ANOTHER COMPLETELY CRAZY JOURNEY THAT WILL TAKE US FAR AND WIDE – FROM THE ROBOT CITY TO THE LAND OF THE LEPRECHAUNS; FROM THE INCREDIBLE CRYSTAL CRATER TO AN ANCIENT SHIPWRECK!

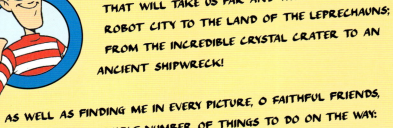

AS WELL AS FINDING ME IN EVERY PICTURE, O FAITHFUL FRIENDS, THERE ARE AN UNBELIEVABLE NUMBER OF THINGS TO DO ON THE WAY: GAMES TO PLAY, TONGUETWISTERS TO SAY, RIDDLES TO SOLVE AND FACTS TO LEARN. AMONG THE CROWDS YOU WILL SPOT A FEW OLD FACES – LOOK OUT FOR WIZARD WHITEBEARD, WOOF AND WENDA; DON'T LET THAT VILLAIN ODLAW SNEAK PAST AND REMEMBER TO LOOK OUT FOR 5 SCROLLS ON THE WAY.

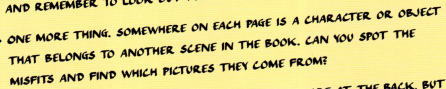

ONE MORE THING. SOMEWHERE ON EACH PAGE IS A CHARACTER OR OBJECT THAT BELONGS TO ANOTHER SCENE IN THE BOOK. CAN YOU SPOT THE MISFITS AND FIND WHICH PICTURES THEY COME FROM?

THE ANSWERS TO ALL THE RIDDLES AND PUZZLES ARE AT THE BACK, BUT NO CHEATING! AND IF YOU'RE NOT TOO WORN OUT BY THE END, EACH PAGE HAS ITS OWN CHECK LIST OF 10 THINGS TO FIND!

OK, LET'S GO, WALLY-WATCHERS! THERE ARE MANY WORLDS OF WEIRD AND WACKY WONDERMENT AWAITING US!

Wally

RAMSHACKLE ROBOTS

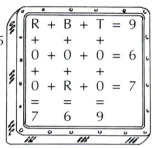

DID YOU KNOW?

The word "robot" comes from the Czech word *robota*, meaning "forced labour". It was first used to describe a mechanical man by a Czech playwright called Karel Capek in 1923.

The world's smallest moving robot is tinier than a sugar cube.

A steam-driven pigeon robot was made in Ancient Greece almost 2,000 years ago.

THINGS TO DO

In this robot-code, all the letters have a different number value and each word has the value of the letters added together.

Here's a clue:

H = 8, A = 7, T = 5

so the word HAT is 8 + 7 + 5 = 20. Look at the code-grid and work out the value of the word ROBOT.

R	+	B	+	T	=	9
+		+		+		
O	+	O	+	O	=	6
+		+		+		
O	+	R	+	O	=	7
=		=		=		
7		6		9		

Why was the robot being silly?   Because he had a screw loose.

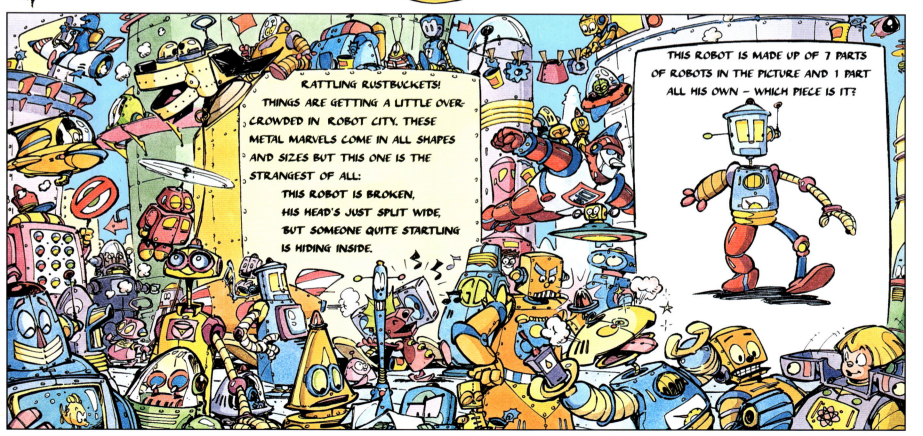

RATTLING RUSTBUCKETS! THINGS ARE GETTING A LITTLE OVER-CROWDED IN ROBOT CITY. THESE METAL MARVELS COME IN ALL SHAPES AND SIZES BUT THIS ONE IS THE STRANGEST OF ALL:

THIS ROBOT IS BROKEN, HIS HEAD'S JUST SPLIT WIDE, BUT SOMEONE QUITE STARTLING IS HIDING INSIDE.

THIS ROBOT IS MADE UP OF 7 PARTS OF ROBOTS IN THE PICTURE AND 1 PART ALL HIS OWN – WHICH PIECE IS IT?

POOLSIDE PARADISE

DID YOU KNOW?

The Romans used to wear leather bikinis.

Tarzan actor Johnny Weismuller won 5 Olympic gold medals for swimming. He built a home in Hollywood with a swimming-pool all round it!

The largest swimming-pool in the world is 5 times larger than a football pitch.

THINGS TO DO

After the pool was drained, 6 things were found at the bottom. Work out what they were by matching the right missing letters to add to the boxes.

wtch	bnn	bt	sndwch	wg	trnks

| aaa | u | a | i | oo | ai |

Where do ghouls most like to swim?

Off the South Ghost.

WHAT A LOT OF HAPPY HOLIDAY-MAKERS! AND I'M HERE TOO SOMEWHERE, ENJOYING THE SUN AND FUN. TALKING OF FUN, CAN YOU FIND THIS CHARACTER? I HOPE HE KNOWS WHAT HE'S DOING:
HE'S GOT 6 SHINY BUTTONS AND A TRAY IN HIS HAND;
A SKATEBOARD,
A RUBBER RING,
WHERE WILL HE LAND?

FIND WHERE EACH OF THESE PIECES COMES FROM IN THE PICTURE AND SPOT THE ONLY ONE THAT MATCHES EXACTLY.

A B C D E F

MOVE ALONG, FRIENDS,
FOR SOME MUSHROOM MAGIC. THEY
LIKE TO GROW IN DARK, DAMP PLACES
SO THIS CHAP IS BEING VERY USEFUL:
I'M WAY UP HIGH,
SMILING DOWN ON THEM ALL,
I TIP UP MY CAN
AND WATCH THE DROPS FALL.

HELP THIS
MUSHROOM FIND HIS CAP.

MUSHROOM MAGIC

DID YOU KNOW?

The stinkhorn fungus of Brazil can grow at the rate of 5 mm a minute. It reaches full size in 20 minutes.

Only 10 % of a mushroom appears above ground. The rest is a network of tiny strands winding through the ground.

Some forest fungi keep growing for hundreds of years and can end up weighing 100 tonnes – as much as a blue whale.

THINGS TO DO

Here are 5 pieces of picture. Three belong to this page and 2 come from somewhere else in the book. Can you find exactly where?

A

B
C

D

E

Which room can't you enter?

ɯoouɥsnɯ ∀

SHOPPING HORROR

CAN YOU FIND 7 OF THESE
OBJECTS IN THE SHOPPING CENTRE?
WHICH 2 ARE MISSING?

DID YOU KNOW?

 The world's largest shopping centre occupies the same amount of space as 58 football pitches.

Escalators rise at a maximum speed of 2.1 km/h.

THINGS TO DO

 Wenda is off to the shops. She has to buy one thing in each of these places:

CLOTHES STORE, TOYSHOP, SPORTS SHOP, FOOD STORE.

 She must visit them in the order shown on the list. Unjumble the muddled words to work out what she had to buy where and which store is which. Then work out the route Wenda took, if she didn't retrace her steps once.

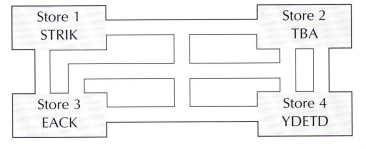

Store 1 STRIK		Store 2 TBA
Store 3 EACK		Store 4 YDETD

When is a shop like a boat?

When it has sales.

CRYSTAL CRATER

DID YOU KNOW?

The largest uncut diamond in the world was called the Cullinan. It weighed over ½ kg and was the size of a man's fist.

Rubies are rarer and more valuable than diamonds.

If all the gold mined since the Stone Age were gathered together, it would create a cube with a base the size of a tennis court!

THINGS TO DO

Here are 7 things people have mined. Unscramble the words and put them into the grid to get the name of a beautiful green gemstone.

DEAJ

OGLD

EMBLAR

PRASIPHE

ALOP

LOCA

MONDIDA

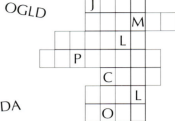

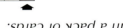

Where's the easiest place to find diamonds?   In a pack of cards.

I'M SUPPOSED TO BE JUDGING THIS COOKING COMPETITION BUT TEMPERS ARE RUNNING SHORT. CAN YOU FIND THIS TROUBLEMAKER? HE'S GOT A HUGE SMILE AND HE'S WEARING A HAT, HE'S HIDDEN A SLICE, IT'S BEHIND HIS BACK.

FIND THE RIGHT PATH THROUGH THE MAZE TO REACH THE CHERRY AT THE OTHER SIDE.

COOKING COMPETITION

DID YOU KNOW?

The red food colouring cochineal is made from the dried bodies of small South American insects.

Cheese was used as a medicine in Ancient Greece.

According to legend, King Alfred the Great got into trouble when he forgot to keep an eye on a peasant woman's cakes in the oven and let them burn!

THINGS TO DO

The Amazing Biscake (half biscuit, half cake!)

You will need: 75 g sugar, 75 g butter, 1 tbsp drinking chocolate, an egg, a 300 g packet of crisp tea biscuits.

1. Put the biscuits in a plastic bag and crush using a rolling-pin.
2. Beat the egg in a bowl and put it into a saucepan with the sugar, drinking chocolate and butter. Melt over a low heat and keep stirring until the mixture boils. Then take it off the heat.
3. Add the biscuits, mix and leave to cool.
4. Mould the mixture into any shape you like. Put it in the fridge to get really cold and then eat it!

Why are cooks cruel?   *Because they whip cream and beat eggs.*

SNAKY GAMES

DID YOU KNOW?

After eating a large animal, a python may not need to eat again for over a month.

One boa constrictor is known to have lived for over 40 years.

Pit vipers have heat sensitive cells in their heads and they can sense the warmth of a small animal's body several metres away in the dark.

THINGS TO DO

Here are 3 slippery snake tongue-twisters. Say them as fast as you can without tying your tongue in knots!

My sister constrictor constricts a constructor.

Five vile vipers filing.

I saw seven saucy snakes slither sideways.

What happened to the snake with a cold?   *She had to viper nose.*

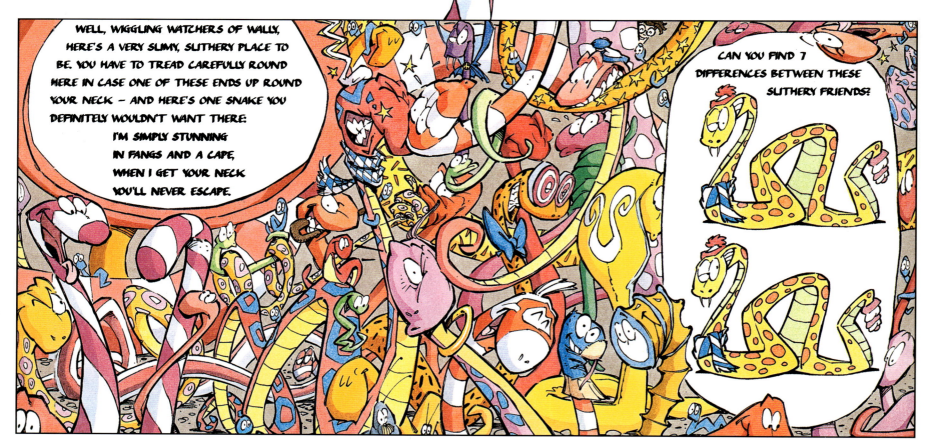

WELL, WIGGLING WATCHERS OF WALLY, HERE'S A VERY SLIMY, SLITHERY PLACE TO BE. YOU HAVE TO TREAD CAREFULLY ROUND HERE IN CASE ONE OF THESE ENDS UP ROUND YOUR NECK – AND HERE'S ONE SNAKE YOU DEFINITELY WOULDN'T WANT THERE. I'M SIMPLY STUNNING IN FANGS AND A CAPE, WHEN I GET YOUR NECK YOU'LL NEVER ESCAPE.

CAN YOU FIND 7 DIFFERENCES BETWEEN THESE SLITHERY FRIENDS?

THESE POOR KNIGHTS HAVE GOT LOST IN THE WOODS AND ARE NOW IN A SPOT OF TROUBLE, O FAITHFUL FOLLOWERS OF WALLY. THIS ONE HAS CERTAINLY GOT MORE THAN HE BARGAINED FOR:

I'M CAUGHT IN A TRAP
AND BOUND IN GREEN ROPE.
FOR A CHANCE OF ESCAPE
I HAVEN'T A HOPE.

ONLY 2 OF THESE HELMETS ARE IDENTICAL. CAN YOU FIND WHICH ONES?

A B C
D E F
G

FOREST FUN

DID YOU KNOW?

Some trees can communicate with each other. If hungry caterpillars attack one, it will produce a chemical which makes it impossible for the caterpillars to digest. Other trees nearby, which are not even touching the attacked tree, sense the chemical in the air and start producing it too.

THINGS TO DO

The leader of the knights has sent an urgent message to his troops in hidden vowel-code. Can you decipher it using this key?

A	E	I	O	U
X	Y	Z	K	I

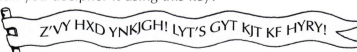

Z'VY HXD YNKJGH! LYT'S GYT KJT KF HYRY!

Now decipher this code to learn which knight is the leader.

HY HXS X GKLD HYLMYT WZTH XN KRXNGY FYXTHYR.

What makes a tree noisy?

Its bark.

HELP JIM THE LEPRECHAUN FIND HIS WAY TO THE COIN BEFORE HIS FRIENDS BEAT HIM TO IT.

LUDICROUS LEPRECHAUNS

DID YOU KNOW?

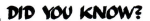

In Irish folklore, a leprechaun is a fairy who looks like a tiny old man, wearing a cocked hat and leather apron. Leprechauns are nearly always found making a single shoe.

If you capture a leprechaun you can force him to reveal his crock of gold, as long as you don't take your eyes off him.
He will try to trick you into looking away, and if you do he will vanish.

A four-leafed clover is not only lucky, it also protects the finder from fairy magic.

THINGS TO DO

The Leprechaun's Coin Trick

You need 3 coins, a pencil and some paper. Draw a straight line down the middle of the paper.
Now, can you place the coins so that there are 2 heads on one side of the line and 2 tails on the other side?
It's easier than you think!

What bow can't be tied?   ˙ʍoquᴉɐɹ ∀

EASTER PARADE

DID YOU KNOW?

The Easter bunny was originally the hare, which was linked to pagan spring festivals and the moon goddess.

The longest rabbit ears found were 71 cm long.

A single pair of rabbits could produce a family of 33 million animals in only 3 years if all their offspring survived.

THINGS TO DO

There are more words than you might expect hidden in an:

EASTER BUNNY

How many can you find?

20, good;
30, very good;
over 50, really remarkable!

What do you call a naughty egg?

A practical yolker.

SPRING HAS SPRUNG, WALLY-WATCHERS AND IT'S TIME FOR PAINTED EGGS AND RIOTOUS RABBITS. HERE'S ONE: HE'S PAINTED AN EGG WITH A STRANGE YELLOW FACE, BUT THE LITTLE WHITE RABBIT THINKS IT LOOKS OUT OF PLACE.

WHICH PIECE OF CRACKED SHELL WILL COMPLETE THE EGG?

TROJAN ELEPHANT

DID YOU KNOW?

The legend is that the Greeks besieged the city of Troy for 10 years. At last, the hero Odysseus had the idea of building a giant wooden horse and filling it with soldiers. It was left outside the gates and when the Trojans brought it in, the Greek soldiers crept out.

The Egyptian Pharaoh Psamtik I besieged the city of Azotus in Israel for 29 years in the 7th century BC. He could have done with a wooden horse!

THINGS TO DO

All these mixed up words can be found in the picture. Unjumble the letters to fill the grid, then read down the middle column to find out how I eventually escaped from the scene.

HLIEDS

PARES

GEESI

RIFE

SLAWL

DORIELS

What game do elephants play in a car?

Squash.

VEGETABLE MATTERS

DID YOU KNOW?

Potatoes were eaten in South America as long ago as 200 AD.

The durian, a fruit from south-east Asia, is the world's smelliest fruit, but it is also very delicious.

Tomatoes were first eaten as fruit, and not used like vegetables until the 19th century.

THINGS TO DO

The Great Fruit and Veg Maze

Hidden in this maze are 3 fruit and vegetables which have been split into two. Match up the halves, shading in the boxes as you do so.
Then trace a path through the maze using just the shaded letters.
Which letter do you come to?

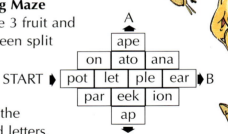

		A ▲		
		ape		
	on	ato	ana	
START ▶ pot	let	ple	ear	▶ B
	par	eek	ion	
		ap		
		▼ C		

What's round, brown and giggles?

A tickled onion.

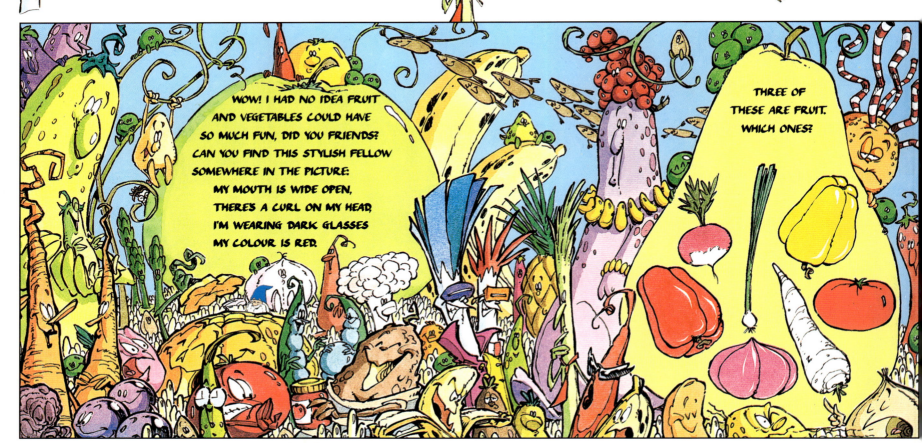

WOW! I HAD NO IDEA FRUIT AND VEGETABLES COULD HAVE SO MUCH FUN, DID YOU FRIENDS? CAN YOU FIND THIS STYLISH FELLOW SOMEWHERE IN THE PICTURE: MY MOUTH IS WIDE OPEN, THERE'S A CURL ON MY HEAD, I'M WEARING DARK GLASSES MY COLOUR IS RED.

THREE OF THESE ARE FRUIT. WHICH ONES?

BEACH DELIGHTS

DID YOU KNOW?

Polynesian islanders believed the sound you heard if you put a seashell to your ear was the voice of a god living inside.

 A giant clam contains enough meat to provide a meal for 4 people.

Only 1 oyster in 1,000 actually contains a pearl and it takes 6 years for a pearl to form.

THINGS TO DO

Find your way from sea to sun by following the clues to each word and changing one letter each time.

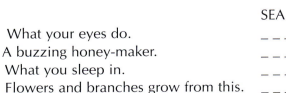

What your eyes do.
A buzzing honey-maker.
What you sleep in.
Flowers and branches grow from this.
A hot cross cake.

What is the best day to go to the beach?

SEA
_ _ _
_ _ _
_ _ _
_ _ _
_ _ _
SUN

Sun-day.

SNOW SCULPTING

DID YOU KNOW?

No two snowflakes are exactly the same.

About $\frac{1}{10}$ of the Earth is permanently covered by ice, mostly in Antarctica and Greenland. If it all melted, the sea would rise by 60 m, drowning many large cities, including New York, London and Tokyo.

A glacier in Greenland moves as much as 19 m every day.

THINGS TO DO

Can you match the silhouettes to their originals?
Only 3 come from this page; the others can be found somewhere else in the book – can you find where?

What do you sing on a snowman's birthday?

„Freeze a jolly good fellow."

WOW! IT LOOKS AS THOUGH THESE STRANGE SNOWMEN ARE A LITTLE BORED WITH THEIR NORMAL SHAPES AND ARE EXPERIMENTING WITH NEW DESIGNS! AND CAN YOU SPOT THIS CLUMSY FELLOW? HE'S LEARNING TO JUGGLE, THERE'S A LONG WAY TO GO, ON HIS HEAD SOME SQUASHED FRUIT HAS COVERED THE SNOW.

WHICH 2 OF THESE THINGS DO NOT APPEAR IN THE PICTURE?

I'M SURE EVERY WALLY-WATCHER ENJOYS A GOOD PILLOW FIGHT FROM TIME TO TIME BUT THESE NIGHT-TIME KNIGHTS HAVE TAKEN THINGS A BIT FAR. CAN YOU SEE THIS CHAP WHO IS ALL READY FOR BED?

HE'S CLEANED HIS TEETH, YOU CAN TELL BY HIS SMILE, THEY'RE GLEAMING AND WHITE AND STAND OUT HALF A MILE.

YOU'VE HEARD OF COUNTING SHEEP, WELL, TRY COUNTING THESE PILLOWS BELOW AND SEE HOW TIRED IT MAKES YOU.

PILLOW FIGHT PARTY

 ## THINGS TO DO

DID YOU KNOW?

Every night you grow about 8 mm as your spine relaxes. During the day you shrink again!

Some sloths and armadillos spend up to 80 % of their lives asleep.

The largest bed ever built was big enough for 39 people.

What is hidden in this giant bedsock?

Why did the man put his bed in the fireplace?

Because he wanted to sleep like a log.

IF THESE DIVERS THINK THEY'RE
GOING TO GET HOME WITH LOTS OF LONG
LOST TREASURE THEY'VE GOT ANOTHER THING
COMING — THE SEA CREATURES ARE DOING WHAT
THEY CAN TO STOP THEM AND HAVING GREAT FUN AT
THE SAME TIME. LOOK AT THIS HAPPY ANIMAL:

I'M HIGH ON A LEDGE,
I'M SMILING AND BROWN,
IF I GRAB HIS LONG AIR PIPE
THIS DIVER WILL FROWN.

CAN YOU FIND ME IN MY UNDERWATER GEAR,
WALLY-WATCHERS?

CAN YOU PUT THESE THINGS FROM THE PICTURE INTO 5 RELATED PAIRS?

WHAT A WRECK!

DID YOU KNOW?

The oldest shipwreck ever found was a Bronze Age ship over 3,000 years old.

The Spanish Armada, which attacked Britain in 1588, was thought to be invincible. By the time it returned home, 70 of its 130 ships had been sunk, mostly because of bad weather.

The deepest part of the ocean is the Mariana's Trench in the Pacific. It is 10,916 m deep, which is the depth of 28 Empire State Buildings on top of each other.

THINGS TO DO

Here is a map of the old wreck. There are 7 treasures inside but also a SHARK, an OCTOPUS, a JELLYFISH and a CRAB. Only the crab is safe to go near. Which three treasures can you bring out of the wreck, if you can't go in the rooms with the dangerous creatures?

The treasures are: PEARLS, SWORD, KEY, CHEST, GEM, COINS, RING.

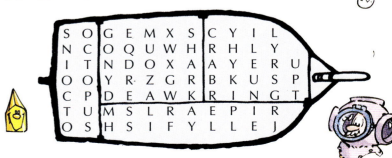

S	O	G	E	M	X	S	C	Y	I	L
N	C	O	Q	U	W	H	R	H	L	Y
I	T	N	D	O	X	A	A	Y	E	R	U
O	O	Y	R	Z	G	R	B	K	U	S	P
C	P	D	E	A	W	K	R	I	N	G	T
T	U	M	S	L	R	A	E	P	I	R
O	S	H	S	I	F	Y	L	L	E	J

What do you call a baby crab?

A nipper.

MUSHROOM MAGIC

- A shouting mushroom
- A cheese-headed mushroom
- 2 umbrella caps
- A red bow
- 3 floating mushrooms
- A mushroom in sunglasses
- 5 stripy cap mushrooms
- A mushroom on a broomstick
- 9 tiny red cap mushrooms
- An axe

COOKING COMPETITION

- A twin-headed monster
- A very hot cake
- A carrot cake
- An outer-space cake
- 7 little frogs
- An explorer
- A cross girl
- 4 balloons
- A giant mouse
- 7 cherries with stalks

RAMSHACKLE ROBOTS

- A goldfish
- A can of oil
- A robot with a radio
- A red flag
- A bug in a stripy shirt
- A robot dog
- A robot washing-line
- 2 red arrows
- A helicopter robot
- 8 tin cans

SHOPPING HORROR

- A hammer
- A boy with a radio
- A pink handbag
- A shopper on a skateboard
- A bird in a nest
- 2 red and white bobble hats
- A teddy in a bow tie
- A happy baby
- A pink mouse
- 10 silver coins

SNAKY GAMES

- A blue and white scarf
- A winking snake
- A starry snake body
- A blue and white hat
- A fake head on a tail
- A walking-stick
- A concertina snake
- A blue bow tie
- A pink-spotted snake
- 13 baby blue snakes

POOLSIDE PARADISE

- An octopus
- A shark
- A flying saucer
- A toy boat
- A man up a tree
- A periscope
- A noisy seagull
- A pair of green flippers
- A running waiter
- A crocodile head

CRYSTAL CRATER

- A crystal moustache
- A heart
- 2 hammers
- A stone sculptor
- A stone with a long nose
- 2 chisels
- A stone with matches
- A stone with a black eye
- A stone landing on a stone
- 8 ruby people

FOREST FUN

- A mud man in a helmet
- 2 stones tied to arrows
- A tree with a hole
- A yellow knight upside-down
- A stunned mud man
- 2 dogs with stripy tails
- A forest woman with a shield
- 2 stripy knights
- A large blue helmet
- 3 red plumes

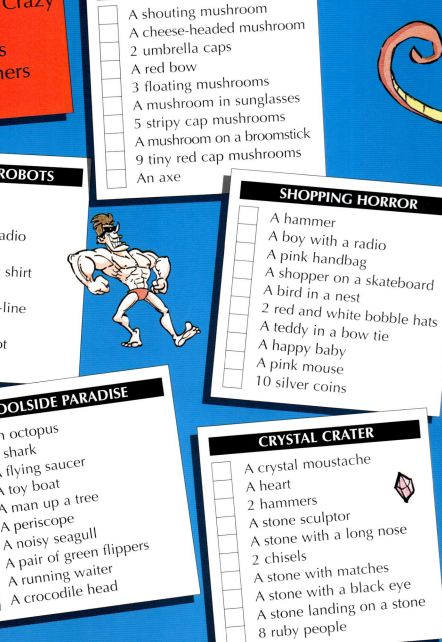
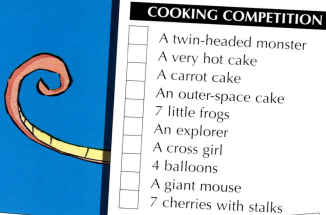
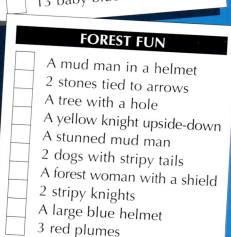